Fetch the Slipper

Sheila Lavelle

Illustrated by
Paula Martyr

PUFFIN BOOKS

PUFFIN BOOKS

Published by the Penguin Group
Penguin Books Ltd, 27 Wrights Lane, London W8 5TZ, England
Penguin Books USA Inc., 375 Hudson Street, New York, New York 10014, USA
Penguin Books Australia Ltd, Ringwood, Victoria, Australia
Penguin Books Canada Ltd, 10 Alcorn Avenue, Toronto, Ontario, Canada M4V 3B2
Penguin Books (NZ) Ltd, 182–190 Wairau Road, Auckland 10, New Zealand

Penguin Books Ltd, Registered Offices: Harmondsworth, Middlesex, England

First published by Hamish Hamilton 1989
Published in Puffin Books 1995
1 3 5 7 9 10 8 6 4 2

Text copyright © Sheila Lavelle, 1989
Illustrations copyright © Paula Martyr, 1989
All rights reserved

PRINTED IN BELGIUM BY
INTERNATIONAL BOOK PRODUCTION

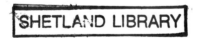

Grandad came downstairs one morning
looking very cross and grumpy.

He looked as grumpy as a giraffe with
a sore throat.

"I've lost one of my slippers," he
grumbled. "One of my best red velvet
slippers, that Betty sent from America.
Now what am I going to do?"

"Put your wellies on instead," said Mum.

Grandad scowled.

"Ha-ha! Very funny," he said. "You're some help, I must say!"

He sat down at the kitchen table.

Jamie and Fiona giggled into their cornflakes.

Dad poured some tea into Grandad's cup.

"Don't worry, Grandad," he said. "Benbow will find it."

Grandad scowled. "Benbow?" he said. "What, him? He's the stupidest dog in the world."

"He's very good at finding things," said Mum.

She gave Grandad a plate of bacon and eggs.

Jamie and Fiona began to shout,
"Benbow! Benbow! Where are you?"

A big collie dog with muddy paws came
running in from the garden.

He was black and white and brown,
with a bushy tail that never stopped
wagging.

Benbow liked fetching things better
than anything else in the world.

"Fetch the slipper, Benbow," said Grandad.

Benbow wagged his tail.

He ran happily out of the kitchen and bounded up the stairs.

Benbow was back in no time with a red velvet slipper in his mouth.

"I told you so," said Mum smugly.

Grandad looked at the slipper.

"That's the left slipper, you mutt!" he said. "It's the right one that's missing!"

Fiona giggled so much she almost choked.

Grandad flung the slipper on the floor.

Jamie buttered a slice of toast.

"Try again, Benbow," he said. "Fetch the *other* slipper."

Benbow raced out again.

He was back in no time with Jamie's
old green shirt that had no buttons on.

"I haven't seen that for years!" laughed
Jamie. "Fetch the SLIPPER, Benbow."

With a joyful bark Benbow dashed
upstairs.

This time he came back with a pink plastic lavatory brush.

"I've been looking for that for weeks!" said Mum in amazement.

Everybody laughed and Benbow galloped out again.

He came back a minute later with
Dad's red woolly nightcap.
"Now where on earth did he find that?"
said Dad, scratching his head.

"FETCH THE SLIPPER, BENBOW!"
everybody shouted together, and Benbow
raced out once more.

This was the best game he had ever
played in his life.

Soon Benbow had made a huge pile of things on the kitchen floor.

He was puffing and panting and his tongue was hanging out of his mouth.

But he still hadn't found Grandad's slipper.

Jamie put his arms round Benbow's neck.

He looked straight into the dog's eyes.

"Slipper, Benbow!" he said. "Slipper! Fetch the SLIPPER!"

Benbow looked at Jamie, his head on one side.

Suddenly Benbow turned and raced out of the kitchen door.

He galloped down the garden path.

He leaped over the gate and bounded down the lane towards the village.

NOW he knew what everybody wanted.

"What on earth can he be up to?" said Mum, pouring another cup of tea.

"Something stupid, I'll bet," grumbled Grandad.

Jamie and Fiona went out into the garden to wait for Benbow to come back.

21

They didn't have to wait long.
Benbow came flying over the garden
gate and raced towards the house.
Something was dangling from his jaws.
Something brown and slippery.
"What can it be?" said Fiona.

Benbow sat down proudly at Jamie's feet.

Jamie took the slippery brown thing out of the dog's mouth.

He laughed so much he almost fell over.

"That's not a slipper, Benbow," he said. "It's a KIPPER!"

"Yuck!" said Fiona, making a face.

Mum gave the kipper to the cat.

"I told you Benbow was a stupid dog," snorted Grandad.

He sat in his old armchair and sulked.

Benbow looked sad and hung his head.
Jamie felt sorry for him.

"Never mind, Benbow," he said. "You
did your best. Let's go and play in the
garden."

Jamie threw Benbow's rubber ball down the lawn and Benbow brought it back.

"Good dog!" said Jamie.

Benbow wagged his tail.

"My turn now," said Fiona.

She threw the ball.

This time it didn't roll over the grass.

It bounced through the kitchen doorway and rolled under Grandad's chair.

"What a rotten throw!" said Jamie.

"Fetch the ball, Benbow," said Fiona.
Benbow ran into the kitchen.

He lay on the floor and put his head
under Grandad's chair.
He wriggled out with something in his
mouth.

It wasn't the ball.

It was Grandad's lost slipper.

The red velvet one that Betty had sent
from America.

It had been under Grandad's chair all
the time.

"Grandad!" laughed Jamie. "Benbow
has found your slipper!"

Everybody hugged and patted Benbow.

Even Grandad began to smile.

"He's the cleverest dog in the world," he said. "Haven't I always said so?"

Also available in First Young Puffin

THE DAY THE SMELLS WENT WRONG
Catherine Sefton

It is just an ordinary day, but Jackie and Phil can't understand why nothing smells as it should. Toast smells like tar, fruit smells like fish, and their school dinners smell of perfume!

Together, Jackie and Phil discover the cause of the problem . . .

DUMPLING
Dick King-Smith

Dumpling wishes she could be long and sausage-shaped like other dachshunds. When a witch's cat grants her wish, Dumpling becomes the longest dog ever.

BELLA AT THE BALLET
Brian Ball

Bella has been looking forward to her first ballet lesson for ages – but she's cross when Mum says Baby Tommy is coming with them. Bella is sure Tommy will spoil everything, but in the end it's hard to know who enjoys the class more – Bella or Tommy!